The Witches

A Winnipesaukee Adventure

DANGER

by Andy Opel

Andy Opel (signature)

illustrated by Karel Hayes

Jetty House • Portsmouth, NH

Dedicated to Alice Bateson Rainie
and
everyone who gets a twinkle in their eye
when they hear, "Let's go to the lake!"

The Witches is set in a time before the majority of Timber Island was established as conservation land. Today Timber Island has three private lots and 126 acres of conservation land that is managed by the Lakes Region Conservation Trust. The conservation easement is designed as a nature preserve and does not allow people to explore the island. Visit www.timberisland.org to learn more about Timber Island.

If you would like to explore an island on Lake Winnipesaukee, the Lakes Region Conservation Trust offers hiking trails on portions of Stonedam, Five Mile, Ragged, Rattlesnake and Blanchard Islands. To learn more about these islands and the Lakes Region Conservation Trust, visit: www.lrct.org

The Lakes Region Conservation Trust was founded in 1979 to conserve the natural heritage of New Hampshire's Lakes Region. LRCT's conservation and stewardship work preserves community character, conserves critical wildlife habitat and diverse ecosystems, protects natural landmarks and scenic landscapes, and provides outdoor recreation opportunities for people of all ages.

© 2011 - Andy Opel - All Rights Reserved. Printed in USA

Second Printing

ISBN 13: 978-0-9828236-6-8
Library of Congress Control Number: 2011927904

Published by
Jetty House
an imprint of
Peter E. Randall Publisher
Box 4726, Portsmouth, NH 03802
www.perpublisher.com

Rough sketches and layout by John Gorey.

www.lakewinniadventures.com

Every summer, they came to Lake Winnipesaukee.

The camp was called Boulder Lodge because of the large rock that sat next to the house.

Franny, J.J., and Jack grew up playing in the water, feeding ducks, and learning all about boats. J.J. was the youngest, and always had to work hard to keep up with his big sister and brother.

When Jack turned eleven, his parents bought him a small boat with a four-horsepower outboard motor.

Jack took J.J. and Franny for rides up and down the shore. "Don't go past the point where I can't see you," their grandmother said. "You never know when a strong wind will come up and swamp the boat."

Jack drove the boat. Franny rode in the front and kept a watch out for rocks, and J.J. sat beside his sister.

One day, Jack decided he wanted to take the boat across the bay
to Timber Island.

"We better not," J.J. warned.
"Grammy said we should stay near the house."

"Yeah, and plus we'll never make it past The Witches,"
said Franny.

"The Witches?" asked J.J. "You mean there are real witches out there?"

"Yeah, big ones with long noses with warts and black hats," said Jack.

"Jack, don't tease him," said Franny. "They aren't real witches, they're
just a bunch of rocks," she said, trying to make J.J. feel better.

"I don't care what they are," said J.J. "I don't like witches."

"Don't worry J.J., we can steer around the rocks and then we
can explore Timber Island. There may even be an Indian cave,"
said Jack, convincing his brother.

"And besides, look how calm the lake is," he added as they pulled away from the dock.

"Do you think that's a rain cloud?" J.J. asked, pointing to a dark cloud.

"Stop worrying," said Jack. "Look how calm it is. It's not going to rain."

"See that blinking buoy?" Franny asked. "That is a marker for The Witches."

"I think I see a witch on that rock over there," said Jack.

"Where, where?" asked J.J., looking scared.

"Jack, don't tease him," Franny told her big brother. "J.J., it's just a legend. There aren't real witches, just rocks to watch out for."

They approached Timber Island and Franny spotted
a small sandy beach to land the boat. As they hiked
around the island, a west wind started to blow and a
dark cloud moved over Saunders Bay.

"Blueberries!" Franny yelled,
as she found a bush full of ripe berries.
Jack and J.J. came over and they picked until their
fingers and lips were stained blue.

"Look at this rock!" said Jack as he climbed to the top of a big boulder.
"I bet Indians used this for a lookout."

"What's that sound?" Jack said, as a low rumble came through the trees.

"Look! There goes The Mount," said Franny, as the *Mount Washington* passed between Timber Island and The Witches.

"Come on you guys," said Jack. "It's getting late." He noticed that Saunders Bay was not looking as friendly as it had earlier.

As they pulled away from Timber Island, the wind started pushing the boat and the waves bounced the children up and down. In a flash, a curtain of water moved across the lake, pouring down on them. With the rain came a thick fog and a strong west wind. It was the kind of sudden storm Grammy had always warned them about.

"Jack, I can't see the shore," Franny yelled from the bow.

"I'm getting soaked," whined J.J.

"It's OK, we're headed in the right direction," said Jack, but what he couldn't see was that the wind was blowing them right into The Witches. The buoys were hidden by the fog and rain.

Suddenly, the boat jumped and the motor stopped.

"What was that?" yelled Franny.

"It's them, I see The Witches!" said J.J.

"I think we hit a rock," said Jack, as he tilted the motor up and saw the bent propeller.

Without the motor, the children were helpless. The wind was blowing them straight into the rocks of The Witches.

The noise of the wind and waves crashing against the rocks sounded like someone moaning.

"Franny, grab my hand," the witch said, as she reached toward the boat.

Franny thought, "How does that witch know my name?"

"Franny, J.J., Jack, it's me, Grammy. Grab this rope so we can tow you," Grammy said as she threw a rope to their boat.

Franny realized it was not a witch she saw, but Grammy.

She grabbed the rope and gave the OK sign.

Mr. Fuller's boat was strong and easily towed the children's boat off the rocks and safely home.

"Grammy, you saved us. How did you know where we were?" Jack asked.

"I was so scared I thought you were a witch," said J.J.

"Your grandmother is a very smart woman and knows all about this lake," said Mr. Fuller. "You kids need to listen to her when she says a storm might come up and blow the boat right off the dock."

All three children nodded in agreement. "We promise we won't do that again Grammy," they said.